Grady the Goose

Written By Denise Brennan-Nelson and Illustrated by Michael Glenn Monroe

To Bob for "honking" at me when necessary
and giving me a "lift" whenever I need one.
And to family and friends who "stick together."

Denise

A special thank-you to my father-in-law Mike
who so graciously posed for this book.

Michael

A special thanks to SBP—you epitomize the word "teamwork."
Continue to be the "V"!

Denise and Michael

Text Copyright © 2006 Denise Brennan-Nelson
Illustration Copyright © 2006 Michael Glenn Monroe

Sleeping Bear Press™

310 North Main Street, Suite 300
Chelsea, MI 48118
www.sleepingbearpress.com

THOMSON
GALE

© 2006 Thomson Gale, a part of the Thomson Corporation.

Thomson, Star Logo and Sleeping Bear Press are trademarks
and Gale is a registered trademark used herein under license.

Printed and bound in Canada.

First Edition

10 9 8 7 6 5 4 3 2 1

Library of Congress Cataloging-in-Publication Data

Brennan-Nelson, Denise.
Grady the goose / written by Denise Brennan-Nelson ;
illustrated by Michael Glenn Monroe.
p. cm.
Summary: Grady the goose is left behind when her family leaves to fly to a warmer
climate, but a helpful farmer finds her and reunites her with her parents and siblings.
ISBN 1-58536-282-4
[1. Geese—Fiction. 2. Individuality—Fiction.] I. Monroe, Michael Glenn, ill. II. Title.
PZ7.B75165Gr 2006
[E]—dc22   2006004566

When the sun peeked over the horizon, the soft blanket of fog that covered the lake turned cotton candy pink. Ripples from restless bullfrogs floated on the surface and dragonflies danced on the lily pads.

At the edge of the lake, nestled among the cattails and the wheatgrass, a mother goose sat in the sturdy nest that she had built to hold her eggs. She had laid an unusually large clutch, 12 eggs in all, and carefully kept them warm and dry for 28 days.

Father goose had fiercely guarded the nest to ensure that no harm came to Momma or their unborn babies.

When Momma woke that morning she knew the day had come. She had felt the tiny rumblings beneath her as her babies worked to free themselves from their hard, white shells. After two long days of pecking, the fuzzy, yellow goslings stumbled and wobbled into the world.

All but one.

Worried, Momma nudged the last egg with her beak, looking for a hole or a crack, but there was nothing. Not wanting to upset the others, she tucked the egg back under her and secretly hoped for a miracle.

Momma tidied the nest and preened her babies. She watched with pride as they stretched their wings and became steady on their feet. And she carefully chose a name for each one.

Momma was trying hard not to think about the egg beneath her when she felt a tiny movement. She raised her body and peeked into the nest just as her last gosling was emerging from the shell.

Momma knew immediately what to call her. She would name the new baby after her grandmother who always spoke of nature's miracles.

"Oh, Grady," Momma cried. "You're here!"

"Where else would I be?" Grady asked.

"You silly goose," Momma said. "I was worried about you." Grady wiggled out of her mother's embrace. "Don't worry about me, Mom," she said.

When it was time for their first swim, Momma and Papa lined up their babies and counted them.

1, 2, 3, 4, 5, 6, 7, 8, 9, 10, 11...

They were all there—all but one.

"Where is Grady?" Momma asked.

As Grady teetered off to join her siblings, Momma knew it wouldn't be the last time she would worry about her.

She found Grady playing in the
cattails not far from the nest.

"Please, Grady," Momma said.
"We need to stick together."

The goslings stayed close to each other. Except for Grady! She was so excited she jumped in, swimming and splashing past everyone.

"Please, Grady," her mother warned. "We need to stick together."

The days grew longer and the goslings grew bigger as spring turned into summer.

Momma and Papa proudly paraded their family around the lake. When the sun dipped low, the goslings circled in close to their parents. Momma counted her babies to make sure they were all there.

1, 2, 3, 4, 5, 6, 7, 8, 9, 10, 11...

"Where is Grady?" Momma asked. The chattering crickets had lured Grady to the edge of the lake.

Her father sternly warned her,
"Grady, we need to stick together."

One beautiful day Momma and Papa gathered their goslings together. Today was the day they would learn to fly!

Momma showed them how to flap and use their wings. She told them how they could take turns leading each other. Papa explained how they could use their bodies to protect and help the bird flying behind them.

They practiced taking off and landing, and before Papa led them into the air Momma reminded them, "Stick together."

Fall began sneaking into summer. Before long, the maple trees stood naked and a thin crust of ice began to grow at the edge of the lake.

"It's time to head south," Momma and Papa announced. "Soon the water will be frozen and food will be scarce. We'll start our journey tomorrow."

Early the next day, geese from nearby ponds and lakes gathered in a field to begin their journey south. They each took off, and then came together in one large flock forming a giant **V** in the sky.

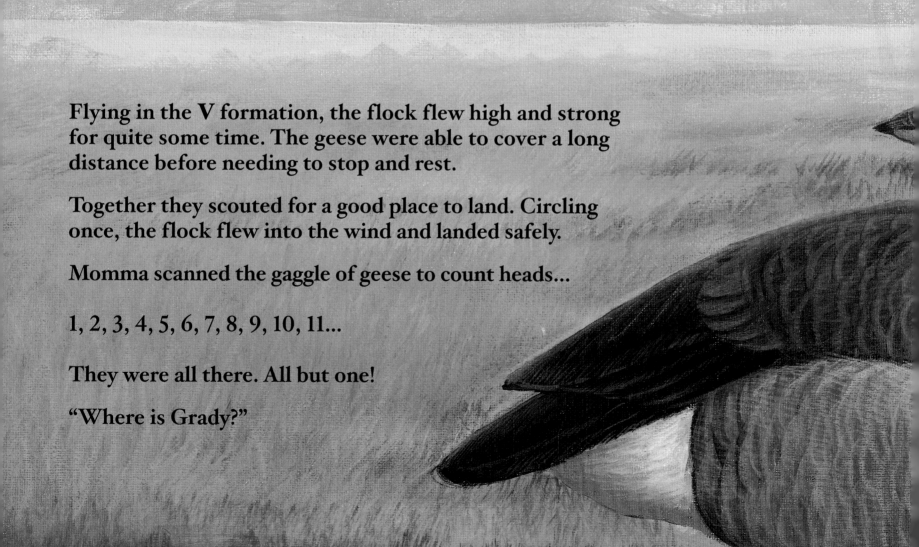

Flying in the **V** formation, the flock flew high and strong for quite some time. The geese were able to cover a long distance before needing to stop and rest.

Together they scouted for a good place to land. Circling once, the flock flew into the wind and landed safely.

Momma scanned the gaggle of geese to count heads...

1, 2, 3, 4, 5, 6, 7, 8, 9, 10, 11...

They were all there. All but one!

"Where is Grady?"

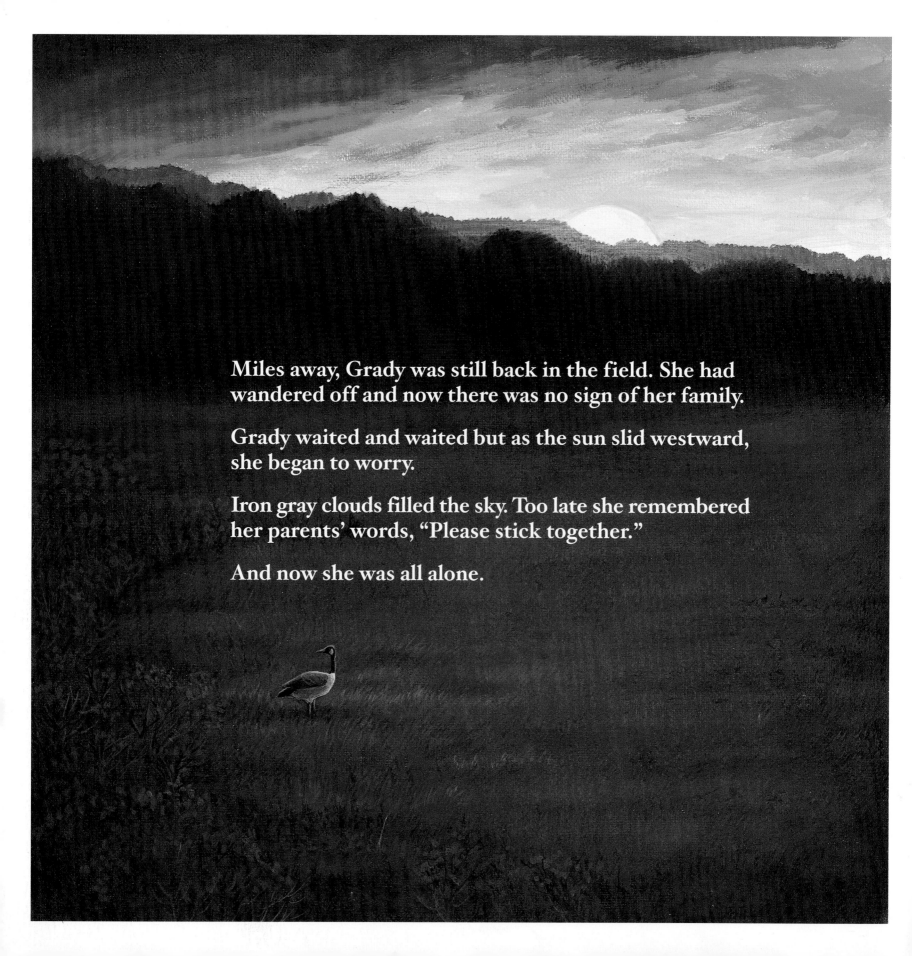

Miles away, Grady was still back in the field. She had wandered off and now there was no sign of her family.

Grady waited and waited but as the sun slid westward, she began to worry.

Iron gray clouds filled the sky. Too late she remembered her parents' words, "Please stick together."

And now she was all alone.

The wind moaned. The grass rustled.

Suddenly... something lunged at her from the shadows.

Grady frantically flapped her wings and escaped into the dark night.

Desperate to find her family, she flew as long and as hard as she could. But the wind was too strong and with no one to help her, she quickly grew tired.

Grady spotted a river. She tried to land in the water but her tired wings gave out and she fell, tumbling in the grass.

She felt something tug at her leg. She tried to pull free but it only tightened its grip.

Throughout the night Grady struggled to free herself. Finally, frightened and exhausted, she collapsed.

"I'll never find my family."

Early the next morning the farm animals were restless. They had heard Grady's cries in the night and they stood facing the direction of the river out beyond the farmhouse.

"What's up, old girls?" The farmer asked his cows. Curious, he walked toward the river.

When he spotted Grady, the farmer approached her carefully and said in a quiet voice, "What are you doing here all alone? I thought geese stuck together."

He bent down and used his jackknife to cut her free. Grady didn't move. He stroked her ruffled feathers.

"Well, you won't get far on your own." Gently, the farmer picked Grady up and carried her to his truck. "Let's see what we can do about that."

The truck rumbled down the road past corn and alfalfa fields, until the farmer found what he was looking for.

The farmer lifted Grady out of the truck and walked to the edge of the field. He set her down and slowly backed away.

Familiar sounds of squawking and honking stirred Grady. When she mustered the strength to raise her head she saw the most beautiful sight she had ever seen.

"Oh, Grady!" Momma cried. "You're here!"

Momma pulled Grady into the warmth
of her soft down feathers.

"Where else would I be?" Grady said.

"After all...we need to stick together."

Facts about Canada Geese

From the Author

The sights and sounds of Canada Geese migrating in "V" formation offer a dramatic display of family bonding and an opportunity to learn from nature.

Scientists believe that geese fly in "V" formation for a few simple but important reasons. The goose in front blocks the wind from those flying behind, giving them a "lift" and making it easier for them to fly. After leading the way and deflecting the wind, a tired goose goes to the back of the line and "rests." By each goose taking its turn as the lead, the flock is able to fly longer distances than if the geese flew alone. They are also able to keep better track of each other, lending help if one gets wounded or sick.

The honking you hear as geese fly overhead is really "goose talk." They communicate with each other about flight speeds and the direction that they are going.

Geese (are able to) fly thousands of miles by working together and sharing the responsibilities. Within our families, our communities, our schools, and the workplace there are many opportunities to follow nature's examples.

**When you see geese in "V" formation,
remember why they fly like they do;
Geese know it's important to stick together
and Grady hopes you do, too.**

Words to Know

Gosling: a young goose
Gaggle: a group of geese on the ground
Skein: a flock of geese, or similar birds, in flight
Clutch: the complete set of eggs produced at one time
Flock: a group of animals that live, travel, or feed together
Preen: to smooth or clean feathers with the beak or bill